# Dear Parents:

Congratulations! Your child is taking the first steps on an exciting journey. The destination? Independent reading!

**STEP INTO READING®** will help your child get there. The program offers five steps to reading success. Each step includes fun stories and colorful art or photographs. In addition to original fiction and books with favorite characters, there are Step into Reading Non-Fiction Readers, Phonics Readers and Boxed Sets, Sticker Readers, and Comic Readers—a complete literacy program with something to interest every child.

## Learning to Read, Step by Step!

**Ready to Read   Preschool–Kindergarten**
• big type and easy words • rhyme and rhythm • picture clues
For children who know the alphabet and are eager to begin reading.

**Reading with Help   Preschool–Grade 1**
• basic vocabulary • short sentences • simple stories
For children who recognize familiar words and sound out new words with help.

**Reading on Your Own   Grades 1–3**
• engaging characters • easy-to-follow plots • popular topics
For children who are ready to read on their own.

**Reading Paragraphs   Grades 2–3**
• challenging vocabulary • short paragraphs • exciting stories
For newly independent readers who read simple sentences with confidence.

**Ready for Chapters   Grades 2–4**
• chapters • longer paragraphs • full-color art
For children who want to take the plunge into chapter books but still like colorful pictures.

**STEP INTO READING®** is designed to give every child a successful reading experience. The grade levels are only guides; children will progress through the steps at their own speed, developing confidence in their reading. The F&P Text Level on the back cover serves as another tool to help you choose the right book for your child.

Remember, a lifetime love of reading starts with a single step!

Visit us on the Web!
StepIntoReading.com
rhcbooks.com

Educators and librarians, for a variety of teaching tools, visit us at
RHTeachersLibrarians.com

*Library of Congress Cataloging-in-Publication Data*
Names: Depken, Kristen L., author. | DiCicco, Sue, illustrator.
Title: The shy little kitten's Christmas / by Kristen L. Depken ; illustrated
by Sue DiCicco.
Description: New York : Random House, [2018] | Series: Step into reading.
Ready to read, step 1 | Summary: At Christmas, six kittens play in the
snow then return home, where the shy little kitten learns that the best
gifts are the ones you give.
Identifiers: LCCN 2017031177 (print) | LCCN 2017042958 (ebook) |
ISBN 978-1-5247-6811-9 (ebook) | ISBN 978-1-5247-6809-6 (pb) |
ISBN 978-1-5247-6810-2 (glb)
Subjects: LCSH: Kittens—Juvenile fiction. | CYAC: Cats—Fiction. |
Animals—Infancy—Fiction. | Snow—Fiction. | Christmas—Fiction.
Classification: LCC PZ10.3.D425 (ebook) | LCC PZ10.3.D425 Sk 2018 (print) |
DDC [E]—dc23

Printed in the United States of America
10 9 8 7 6 5 4 3 2 1

This book has been officially leveled by using the F&P Text Level Gradient™
Leveling System.

STEP INTO READING®

STEP 1 READY TO READ

# THE SHY LITTLE KITTEN'S CHRISTMAS

by Kristen L. Depken
illustrated by Sue DiCicco

Random House 🏠 New York

Six little kittens
are ready
for Christmas.
Black-and-white.
One has stripes.

The mother cat
looks out the window.
Snow!

6

One, two, three,
four, five, six
little kittens
go out to play.

Plop, plop, plop
down the steps!

Roll, roll, roll
down the hill.

"Chirp! Chirp!"
A red bird.

The shy little kitten
follows it.

"Chee! Chee!"

A chubby squirrel.

Hop, hop, hop
over a log.

"Hoot! Hoot!"

A snowy owl.

The wind blows.

<u>Brr!</u>

Where is home?

"Chirp! Chirp!
Follow me!"
Over a log.

19

Up, up, up
the hill.
Look!
In the sky!

Up the steps.
Home at last.
"Thank you,
red bird."

The shy little kitten
is ready for Christmas.

# Now it is
# Christmas morning!

# One green tree.

Five little kittens
add red bows.

The shy little kitten
has a special gift.
Merry Christmas!

# Best Christmas ever!